This book belongs to:

Contents

Cover illustration by Peter Brown

Published by Ladybird Books Ltd
27 Wrights Lane London W8 5TZ
A Penguin Company
3 5 7 9 10 8 6 4

Printed in Italy

Time for school

written by Marie Birkinshaw
illustrated by Tony Kenyon

"Hurry up," said Mum, "or we'll be late for school."

We all rushed downstairs, picked up our bags and went outside. Mum closed the door.

"No, wait!" said Kate.
"I've forgotten my homework.
Mrs James will go mad if I don't
have it with me this time!"

So we all went back inside.

"Be quick, Kate," cried Mum, "or we'll be very late for school, and Mrs James really will be cross with you."

Kate found her homework and
rushed downstairs.
We all picked up our bags and
went outside.
Mum closed the door and
turned the key in the lock.
We all headed for the car.

"No, wait!" said Charlie.
"I've forgotten my sports kit
and it's football today."

So we all went back inside.

"Hurry up, Charlie!" cried
Mum. "We'll be late for school!"

Charlie got his sports kit and rushed downstairs.
We all picked up our bags and went outside.

Mum closed the door and turned the key in the lock. She unlocked the car and we all tried to get in the front seat.

We could tell by the look on Mum's face that this was not a good idea, so we got in the back and put on our seatbelts.

"I don't believe it!" cried Mum.
"I've forgotten my bag!
We'll never get to school
at this rate."

She took off her seatbelt and
went back in the house.

Mum found her bag and rushed out of the front door.

She locked the door, got back into the car, put on her seatbelt and started the car up.

"Can we have the radio on, please, Mum?" said Kate.

"OK," said Mum. "But let's get going or we'll never get to school today."

And the man on the radio said,

Good morning! Now for the latest news on this lovely Saturday morning...

Saturday?
I don't believe it!

The ghost house

written by Marie Birkinshaw
illustrated by Peter Brown

This is the door
to the ghost house.

This is the train
that rumbles the floor,
as it goes through the door
to the ghost house.

This is the chain
that rattles the train,
that rumbles the floor,
as it goes through the door
to the ghost house.

This is the hand
that shakes the chain,
that rattles the train,
that rumbles the floor,
as it goes through the door
to the ghost house.

This is the face
that follows the hand,
that shakes the chain,
that rattles the train,
that rumbles the floor,
as it goes through the door
to the ghost house.

This is the scream
that comes from the train
when we see the face
that follows the hand,
that shakes the chain,
that rattles the train,
that rumbles the floor,
as it goes through the door
to the ghost house.

SCREAM!

And this is the way out...

Let's go round again!

The raven and the jug

One of Aesop's fables
illustrated by Peter Massey

A big black raven wanted
a drink.

She saw a big jug with water
at the bottom. But she couldn't
reach the water.

So the raven collected some stones and put them into the jug, one by one.

The water rose up and up the jug until...

At last the raven had
a long, long drink.

Moral: If you try hard enough, you can do things that you thought would be very difficult.

Night flight

written by Catriona Macgregor
illustrated by Andy DaVolls

In the middle of the night,
When the moon is bright
And the lightest of breezes
Are all just right,

Find a branch high up
And hold on tight.
Don't worry at all,
You'll be all right.

Just take a deep breath...
And a step to the right...
Then flap your wings
With all your might.

That's right! You've done it!
Your very first flight.

radio
rate
rattles
raven
reach
rose
rumbles
rushed
scream
seat
seatbelts
shakes
started
step
stones

take
tight
try
wait
whoopee
wings

Level 1 – Start reading

For a child who is at the first reading stage – whether he or she is at school or about to start school. Uses rhyme and repetitive phrases to build sentences and introduces and emphasises important words relating to everyday childhood experiences.

Level 2 – Improve reading

Building on the reading skills taught at home and in school, this level helps your child to practise the first 100 key words. The stories help develop your child's interest in reading with structured texts while maintaining the fun of learning to read.

Level 3 – Practise reading

At this level, your child is able to practise new-found skills and move from reading out loud to independent silent reading. The longer stories and rhymes develop reading stamina and introduce different styles of writing and a variety of subjects. At the end of this level your child will have read around 1000 different words.

Read with Ladybird...

is specially designed to help your child learn to read. It will complement all the methods used in schools.

Parents took part in extensive research to ensure that **Read with Ladybird** would help your child to:

- take the first steps in reading
- improve early reading progress
- gain confidence in new-found abilities.

The research highlighted that the most important qualities in helping children to read were that:

- books should be fun – children have enough 'hard work' at school
- books should be colourful and exciting
- stories should be up to date and about everyday experiences
- repetition and rhyme are especially important in boosting a child's reading ability.

The stories and rhymes introduce the 100 words most frequently used in reading and writing.

These 100 key words actually make up half the words we use in speech and reading.

The three levels of **Read with Ladybird** consist of 22 books, taking your child from two words per page to 600-word stories.

Read with Ladybird will help your child to master the basic reading skills so vital in everyday life.

Ladybird have successfully published reading schemes and programmes for the last 50 years. Using this experience and the latest research, **Read with Ladybird** has been produced to give all children the head start they deserve.

Learning to read with this book

Special features

The ghost house and other stories is ideal for early independent reading. It includes:

- a longer story to build stamina.
- two rhymes for reading fluency and memory.

Planned to help your child to develop his reading by:

- practising a variety of reading techniques such as recognising frequently used words on sight, being able to read words with similar spelling patterns (eg, night/flight), and the use of letter-sound clues.
- using rhyme to improve memory.
- including illustrations that make reading even more enjoyable.